CONTENTS

GW00374361

EJA Publications

USING THE ACCOMPANIMENTS

The Piano Part

The introductions set the speed and character of the tune. They lead straight into the tune, so do not stop or slow down between the introduction and tune. Familiarise the pupils with the sound of the introduction and practice their entry two or three times, counting aloud the beats of the bar preceding their entry.

All the piano accompaniments are copyright J.C. Pitts with the exception of those on pages 42, 46, 47, 49, 55, 64, 67, 69, 74 and 75.

Use of Guitar

Guitar chords usually follow the exact harmony of the piano accompaniment. However the guitar can also use the simplified chord patterns provided for chime bars, and these rarely use more than three chords per tune. See below for explanation.

Chime Bars, etc.

Where suitable the tunes have been provided with chime-bar chord patterns. A simple scheme is used for the chord charts which are intended for teachers to copy onto the blackboard as required. Coloured chalk should be used to help distinguish the different chord letters and arrows, e.g. 'Mocking Bird'.

Mocking Bird

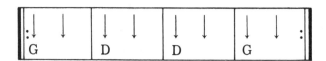

The Chord Chart on page 80 gives details of chords to help teachers to select the correct notes required, e.g. chord G requires the notes G, B, D. It is best to use one child per note, thus chord G requires a group of three children, each holding one chime bar and beater in front of them just below chest height.

On the chart each box represents one bar, and the chords are sounded on each beat of the bar. The arrows show the beats per bàr and the different colours help the children to know when to sound their particular chord. The teacher or a child should point to the arrows in time with the beats to help everyone to keep their place.

For waltz time $\frac{3}{4}$ the relative size of the arrows represents the 'strong-weak-weak' pattern (um-cha-cha) — see below. The root of the chord is sounded first, followed by the remaining notes.

Simple chord patterns have often been possible for chime bars, despite the more complex harmonies of the piano part, by using alternative related chords. E.G. chime bar chord G (notes G, B, D) will harmonise with piano or guitar chord E minor 7 (notes E, G, B, D). Guitarists can play either the guitar or chime-bar chords. Both will fit concurrently with the piano part.

Duets

The book includes 16 duets and of these 10 are for descant and treble recorders together. Another 4 can be used either as treble duets only, or for descant and treble together; the othe 2 duets can only be used by treble recorders. The descant recorder music for 10 of the duets also appears in the descant series 'Recorder from the Beginning' Books 2 and 3 and details are included where appropriate.

CLASS USE WITH SINGERS

Some of the two-part items can be used in class, with treble recorders playing the 2nd part against a 1st group of singers with the optional use of the accompaniments given for pitched and unpitched percussion.

Some suggested items:

Two-part songs
Cudelia Brown
Patapan*
Silent Night*
The Pearly Adriatic*
Santa Lucia*
Pokare Kare*
Cuckoo
Tzena

Rounds
Grand and glorious feeling
Sandy McNab

* No words given.

Sopranino Recorder

As indicated elsewhere, this book can be used to teach sopranino recorder as well as treble recorder. Where this occurs, only six of the duets are usable, i.e. those which are marked as treble duets, this includes the four in which descant recorder is shown to be replaceable by a second treble part.

Zoogie

Ze - bra, Ti - ger, Kan - ga - roo, Snake, Pen - guins, Po - lar Bears, swim-ming in the lake.

Merrily we roll along

Who's that yonder?

The Capucine

French Folk Song

A --

cuck - oo was sing - ing in a tall leaf - y tree. All the

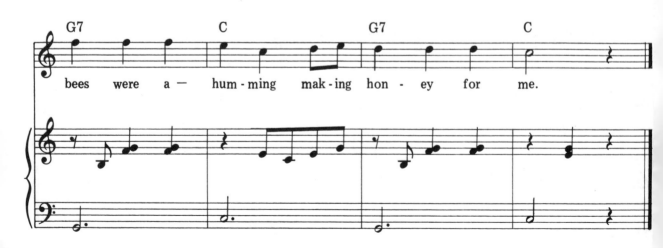

bees were a — hum - ming mak - ing hon - ey for me.

Cobbler's Jig

Irish Lullaby

Two little Angels

The Saints

Add some tambourine accompaniment.

Judge's Dance

The Pearly Adriatic

13

N.B. The Pupil's Book uses a Da Capo instead of the Dal Segno given here.

Teaching point: at the change of time from $\frac{3}{4}$ to $\frac{2}{4}$, try to keep the crotchet speed the same. This will automatically give a feeling of greater speed in the $\frac{2}{4}$ section, followed by a return to the more leisurely $\frac{3}{4}$ opening.

Come hasten, ye shepherds

Suggested accompaniment:

TAMBOURINE — Use this for the first 4 bars and the last 4 bars.

FINGER CYMBALS or SLEIGH BELLS — Use this for the middle section.

Santa Lucia

Don't take this tune too quickly.

Chime bars: these join in at the beginning of the tune.

THREE chords required: C, G7 and F

If you have a bass xylophone, use it to 'double up' the first note of each chime bar chord. You will only need notes C, F and G.

The use of some light percussion will help to emphasise the waltz rhythm. You don't need to use the piano — you could try just bass xylophone and tambourine — or even no accompaniment at all!

TRIANGLE

TAMBOURINE

The descant recorder part of this piece also appears in 'Recorder from the Beginning' Book 3 by John Pitts, pub. Thomas Nelson & Sons Ltd.

Debka hora
(Israeli dance)

Chime bars: THREE chords required: Am, Dm and E7.

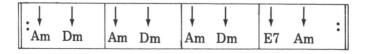

Other parts to add, with or without chime bar chords.

Angie's Jig

Pokare kare

Piano accompaniment: don't go too quickly! Play with a 'swing', slightly accenting the first beat of each bar.

Chime bars: to reduce the number of chords used, chord C is used instead of A minor as well as for its own sake. For Introduction use the last four bars of the chart.

THREE chords required: G, C and D

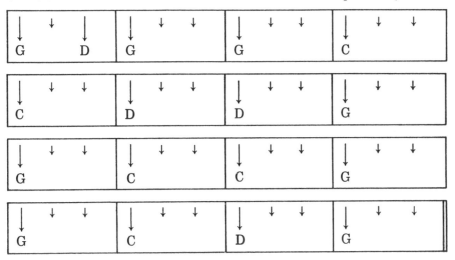

The descant recorder part of this piece also appears in 'Recorder from the Beginning' Book 2 by John Pitts, pub. Thomas Nelson & Sons Ltd.

Cossack Dance

*See page 24 for suggested accompaniment

The descant recorder part of this piece also appears in 'Recorder from the
Beginning' Book 3 by John Pitts, pub. Thomas Nelson & Sons Ltd.

Cossack Dance

Piano accompaniment: don't start off too fast!

Chime bars: for Introduction use the first two bars of the chart, then begin again. Although four chords are used this is *not* too difficult — look at the first two lines. Chord B occurs only once in the whole piece.

FOUR chords required: Am, E7, Dm and B(7)

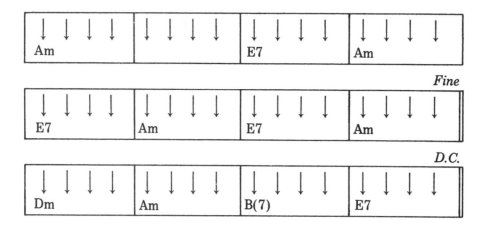

Percussion: on the three occasions that a rest appears in the recorder part, the gap can be helpfully filled with two crotchet (quarter-note) clashes on a tambourine.

The descant recorder part of this piece also appears in 'Recorder from the Beginning' Book 2 by John Pitts, pub. Thomas Nelson & Sons Ltd.

Gay Gordons

Drink to me only.

Arr. © JCP.

26

Czech Polka
(J. Strauss)

Jingle Bells
(James Pierpont)

Jin-gle bells! Jin-gle bells! Jin-gle all the way! Oh what fun it is to ride in a one horse o-pen sleigh. Oh, Jin-gle bells! Jin-gle bells! Jin-gle all the way. Oh, what fun it is to ride in a one horse o-pen sleigh.

Suggestions for accompaniment:

SLEIGH BELLS

TRIANGLE

Both instruments can end with a good rattle (trill) on the last note.

29

Michael, row the boat ashore.

Mi - chael, row the boat a - shore, Al - le - lu - lia, Mi - chael, row the boat a - shore, Al - le - lu - lia.

Alouette
(French song)

He's got the whole world in his hands

N.B. The Pupil's Book uses a Da Capo, despite the Dal Segno needed here.

TWO chords required, C and G7

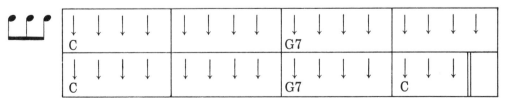

Repeat this chord pattern for the verse.

Silent Night

The descant recorder part of this piece also appears in 'Recorder from the Beginning' Book 3 by John Pitts, pub. Thomas Nelson & Sons Ltd.

Sweet Betsy from Pyke
(American)

(Manx Lullaby — see next page)

Manx Lullaby

Piano introduction: this uses the second line of the recorder tune, so get the children to follow it in their books.

Teaching point: If you want the recorders and chime bars to begin together, get the chime bars to begin with the last chord of line 2 of the chart, and then jump straight back to the beginning of line 1. Count '1 - 2' in the bar in which recorders begin on the third beat. Notice that the recorder and chime bar music uses a Da Capo sign, whilst the piano part requires a Dal Segno.

THREE chords required: G, F and C

↓ ↓ ↓	↓ ↓ ↓	↓ ↓ ↓	↓ ↓ ↓
↓	↓	↓	↓
G	F	G	C

Fine

↓ ↓ ↓	↓ ↓ ↓	↓ ↓ ↓	↓ ↓	↓
↓	↓	↓	↓	↓
G	C		G	G

↓ ↓ ↓	↓ ↓ ↓	↓ ↓ ↓	↓ ↓ ↓
↓	↓	↓	↓
F	G	F	G

D.C.

↓ ↓ ↓	↓ ↓ ↓	↓ ↓ ↓	↓ ↓ ↓
↓	↓	↓	↓
F	G	F	G

'Sweet Betsey from Pyke' — turn to page 35.)

Andante grazioso
(Mozart)

Helston Furry Dance

Cavalry Patrol
(Russian song by Knipper)

Suggestions for accompaniment: a simple part is given for xylophone. Notice that the second line is the same as the first, with the addition of a final bar. Players need to use two beaters!

Rhythm ostinati: point out the way the instruments 'follow' each other, playing alternately.

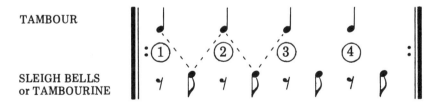

The descant recorder part of this piece also appears in 'Recorder from the Beginning' Book 3 by John Pitts, pub. Thomas Nelson & Sons Ltd.

Minuet
(Purcell)

Dear Liza

Optional rhythm accompaniment: — using (e.g.) claves and maracas or guiro.

The Gospel Train
(Spiritual)

The gos - pel train is com - ing, I hear it just at hand,___ I hear the car wheels mov - ing, And rum - bling thro' the land. Get on___ board, lit - tle

Chime bars: it is best to use two minim (half note) beats per bar for this accompaniment. Notice that the recorders play one note before the chime bars begin.

THREE chords required: G, C and D7

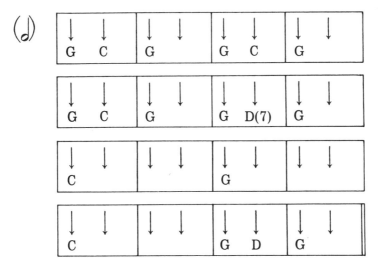

Percussion: a guiro will help to make a good 'train' accompaniment.

Von Himmel hoch
(J. S. Bach)

Emperor's Hymn
(Haydn)

Let the Toast pass
(Scottish)

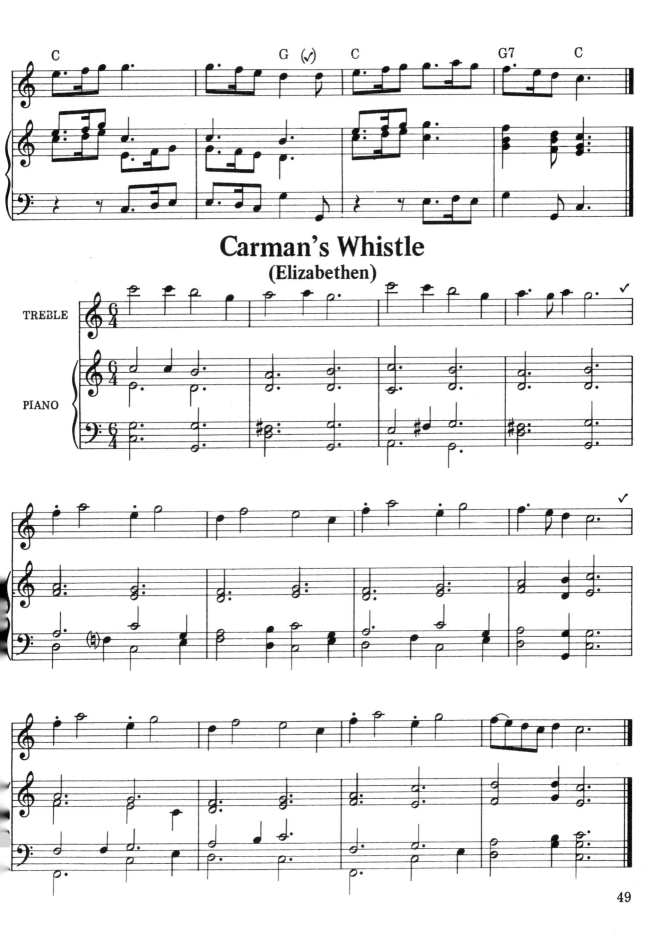

Carman's Whistle

(Elizabethen)

49

Annie Laurie

Old Ark
(Spiritual)

Steal away
(Spiritual)

O Ewigkeit, du Donnerwort
(German hymn)

55

Beckett Blues, One

56 (At written pitch)

This tune uses the traditional twelve-bar blues chord sequence. An alternative piano accompaniment appears in 'Recorder from the Beginning', Teacher's Book 3, along with a companion to this tune, called 'Beckett Blues Two'

Rhythm ostinati: use one or other but not both together.

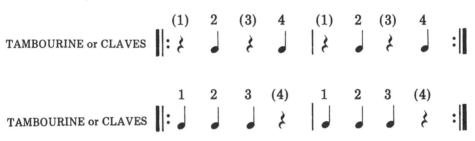

Chime bars: THREE chords required: G, C7 and D

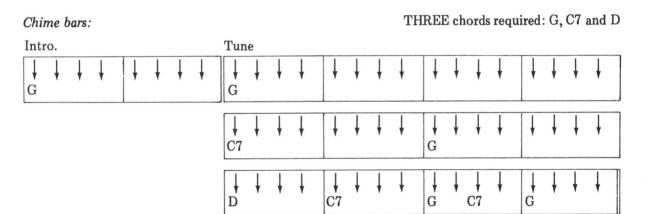

Rigadoon
(Purcell)

This duet for Treble Recorders sounds best unaccompanied. Don't take it too quickly; think of the speed of the fastest section in line 3 before you begin.

Ade, zur guten Nacht
(Farewell, goodnight)

The descant recorder part of this piece also appears in 'Recorder from the Beginning' Book 3 by John Pitts, pub. Thomas Nelson & Sons Ltd.

Cudelia Brown

Arr. © JCP.

The descant recorder part also appears in 'Recorder from the Beginning'
Book 3 by John Pitts, pub. Thomas Nelson & Sons Ltd.

Accompaniment: with or without piano. Try adding these ostinati. Begin
with just the one for maracas. Use the words to help keep in time. When that
is successful add the second ostinato on claves.

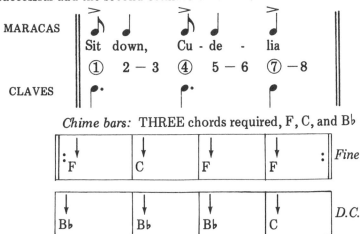

Chime bars: THREE chords required, F, C, and B♭

Chime bars only strike one chord per bar. Omit the repeat when playing the
Da Capo.

Joshua fought the battle of Jericho
(Spiritual)

Josh-ua fought the bat-tle of Jer-i-cho,— Jer-i-cho,— Jer-i-cho,— Josh-ua fought the bat-tle of Jer-i-cho,— And the walls came tum-bling

N.B. The Pupil's Book uses a Da Capo, despite the Dal Segno needed in the piano part.

Play the piece rhythmically and steadily, not too fast.

Cradle Song
(Wiegenlied)
Brahms

The Pupil's Book points out that this piece can be played in two ways:
1. Tune only, for Treble recorders;
2. Duet, for Descant and Treble recorders. Descant recorders play the tune, Trebles play the accompaniment.

Remember that sometimes it is good to have the recorders play a duet *without* piano accompaniment! You might try this here.

Sur le Pont d'Avignon
(French)

Sur le pont d'A - vig - non l'on - y dan - se, l'on - y dan - se,

Sur le pont d'A - vig - non, l'on - y dan - se tout en rond. Les

beaux mes - sieurs font comme - ci. Les bel - les dames font comme ça.

N.B. The Pupil's Book uses a Da Capo instead of the Dal Segno given here.

66

Minuet
(Handel)

Go down, Moses.

(Spiritual)

Air in D minor
(Purcell)

We walk a narrow way
(Israeli)

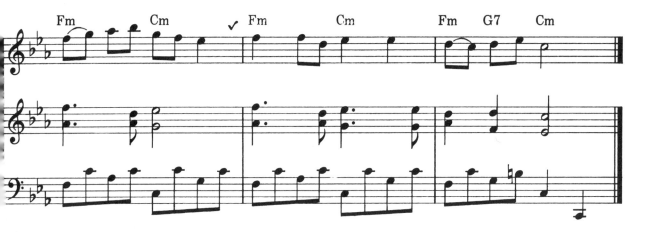

Suggestions for accompaniment: you could add this ostinato on tambourine throughout the first four bars (repeated) and last four bars of the piece. Have a rest for bars five to eight.

TAMBOURINE

A part for pitched percussion is given below:

Patapan
(French)

The descant recorder part of this piece also appears in 'Recorder from the Beginning' Book 3 by John Pitts, pub. Thomas Nelson & Sons Ltd.

Suggestions for accompaniment: the bass ostinato can be played on a drum and/or xylophone. Add a tambourine on the first beat of each bar.

Das neugeborne Kindelein
(Old German hymn)

Herzliebster Jesu
(Old German hymn)

Ball gawn roun'
(Jamaican circle game)

TREBLE

PIANO

De play be-gin an' de ball gawn roun', Maw-ga Nan-ny show me how de ball gawn roun', Play boy, Play boy, Play boy, Play. Maw-ga Nan-ny show me how de ball gawn roun'. King-ston brown gal a-play we de play,

Tzena
(Israeli)

If you wish to use descant recorders instead of trebles for group 1, the
descant music is in 'Recorder from the Beginning' Book 2 by J. Pitts, pub.
Thomas Nelson & Sons Ltd.

Notes required to build chords used on the charts

the chords used are listed here, with details of the particular notes involved. Remember that the notes are listed from lowest note to highest, i.e. the first note listed should be the largest of the chime bars used for that particular chord.

e.g. Chord C uses notes C E G i.e.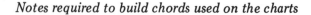

The letter 'm' is an abbreviation for 'minor', thus Dm = D minor. Use of a 7th adds an extra note onto a basic chord, and this extra note can be omitted if desired, e.g. use chord G instead of chord G7.

CHORD	NOTES NEEDED
C(7)	C E G (B♭)
Cm	C E♭ G
D(7)	D F♯ A (C)
Dm	D F A
E♭	E♭ G B♭
E	E G♯ B
Em	E G B
F	F A C

CHORD	NOTES NEEDED
Fm	F A♭ C
G(7)	G B D (F)
Gm	G B♭ D
A(7)	A C♯ E (G)
Am(7)	A C E (G)
B♭	B♭ D F
B(7)	B D♯ F♯ (A)
Bm	B D F♯

Remember that the black notes of a piano can be called either sharps (♯) or flats (♭). A sharp sign ♯ raises a note by a semitone, whilst a flat sign ♭ lowers a note by a semitone. So, e.g. D♯ is the same note as E♭.

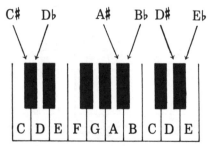

Whether or not we describe a black note as either sharp or flat usually depends upon what key (scale) we are using at the time.